PuRRmaiDs

A Star Purr-formance

by Sudipta Bardhan-Quallen

illustrations by Vivien Wu

A STEPPING STONE BOOK™

Random House 🏠 New York

To Kelly Clarkson, for all the joy
her music brings to my daughter

Text copyright © 2019 by Sudipta Bardhan-Quallen
Cover art copyright © 2019 by Andrew Farley
Interior illustrations copyright © 2019 by Vivien Wu

All rights reserved. Published in the United States by
Random House Children's Books, a division of
Penguin Random House LLC, New York.

Random House and the colophon are registered trademarks and
A Stepping Stone Book and the colophon are trademarks of
Penguin Random House LLC.
PURRMAIDS® is a registered trademark of KIKIDOODLE LLC
and is used under license from KIKIDOODLE LLC.

Visit us on the Web! rhcbooks.com

Educators and librarians, for a variety of teaching tools, visit us at
RHTeachersLibrarians.com

Library of Congress Cataloging-in-Publication Data
Name: Bardhan-Quallen, Sudipta, author.
Title: A star purr-formance / Sudipta Bardhan-Quallen ;
illustrated by Vivien Wu.
Description: First edition. | New York : Random House, 2019. |
Series: Purrmaids ; 5 | "A Stepping Stone Book."
Summary: When purrmaid friends Shelly, Angel, and Coral team up
with the Catfish Club to audition for the annual Founder's Day Showcase,
they learn that singing well requires more than just practice.
Identifiers: LCCN 2018013004 | ISBN 978-0-525-64634-1 (trade pbk.) |
ISBN 978-0-525-64635-8 (lib. bdg.) | ISBN 978-0-525-64636-5 (ebook)
Subjects: | CYAC: Mermaids—Fiction. | Cats—Fiction. | Singing—Fiction. | Festivals—
Fiction. | Friendship—Fiction.
Classification: LCC PZ7.B25007 St 2019 | DDC [Fic]—dc23

Printed in the United States of America
10 9 8 7 6
First Edition

This book has been officially leveled by using
the F&P Text Level Gradient™ Leveling System.

Somehow, every day in Kittentail Cove turned out to be wonderful. There was always something to learn, somewhere to explore, or some adventure to go on. Shelly loved her beautiful underwater town. She couldn't imagine living anywhere else.

"Does anyone know what tomorrow is?" asked Ms. Harbor. She was the teacher in Room Eel-Twelve.

Shelly looked at the small orange kitten to her right. Coral had her paw raised so high she looked like she was going to pop out of her clamshell seat. "I know, I know!" she shouted. "It's Founder's Day!"

"I knew that," Baker grumbled.

"I did, too," Taylor added.

Ms. Harbor laughed. "I guess that wasn't a very hard question!"

"Founder's Day is my favorite day of the year," Coral said.

"It's my favorite, too," Shelly said.

Most of the students nodded in agreement. But not the black-and-white kitten next to Coral. "Founder's Day is my second favorite day of the year," Angel said. "Right after my birthday."

"I'm sure your birthday is a paw-some

day," Ms. Harbor purred. "But we don't have a parade on your birthday."

"We should!" Angel joked.

Most of the class giggled. Shelly rolled her eyes. And Coral sighed, "Oh, Angel!" She shook her head. Angel liked making a splash whenever she could. Sometimes that frustrated Coral, who spent most of her time avoiding splashes.

We're so different, Shelly thought. Coral was a rule-follower and Angel was a rule-breaker. But Shelly wasn't either of those things. She liked rules—as long as she got to decide what those rules were! Somehow, none of that mattered. Angel and Coral had been her best friends fur-ever. Shelly was sure that would never change.

Ms. Harbor held up her paws for

silence. She waited for everyone to settle down. "Maybe next year we can plan a parade for Angel," she said, winking. "But tomorrow's celebrations are in honor of Leondra, the founder of Kittentail Cove. Leondra wanted to build a town where every creature under the sea would be welcome. She hoped that this community

would support each other through good times and bad."

"That's exactly what Kittentail Cove is like!" Shelly said.

Ms. Harbor nodded. "By celebrating Leondra's ideas every year, we remind ourselves to stay that way," she purred. "And there's lots of food!"

The students laughed again. *Ms. Harbor makes every lesson fun,* Shelly thought.

Ms. Harbor continued, "Maybe I'll see some of you out celebrating tomorrow."

"We'll be at the Cove Council party tonight," Baker said.

"My mom says I have to wear a tie," Taylor whined.

"You *should* wear a tie," said Adrianna. She pointed to Umiko and Cascade. "The Catfish Club girls will be dressed up. My uncle, the mayor, expects us to look purr-fect."

Shelly looked away so no one would catch her giggling. Adrianna never missed a chance to tell everyone that her uncle was the mayor of Kittentail Cove.

"We're going to the party, too," Angel said. "Right, Shelly?"

Shelly nodded. "Yes, we'll be there. My parents are making all the food for the party." Her parents owned Lake Restaurant in Kittentail Cove. They were pawsome chefs.

"Now I'll definitely be there tonight!" Ms. Harbor purred. "And I'm sure you're all going to the showcase tomorrow."

The Founder's Day Showcase was a yearly tradition. It was held in the Purr-formance Art Wing, or P.A.W., of the Kittentail Cove Museum. Usually, purrmaids were invited to sing for the entire town. Last year, Katy Purry was the main star. The year before, it was Taylor Shipps.

This year, the Cove Council was trying something new. Instead of inviting just a few purrmaids to sing, they were holding tryouts. Anyone could earn a spot in the purr-formance this year.

"Are any of you planning to audition?" Ms. Harbor asked.

Most of the class shrugged. Except for Adrianna. She was nodding and grinning. "We are!" she exclaimed. "Umiko, Cascade, and I have been practicing."

"Actually," Cascade said, "we've been *planning* to practice. We haven't really sung that much yet."

"Mostly, Adrianna has told us what to do," Umiko said.

Adrianna frowned. "We've almost practiced," she grumbled.

"I tried to get Baker to practice, but it didn't go well," Taylor huffed.

Baker shook his head. "No, it didn't," he agreed.

"Anyone else?" Ms. Harbor asked.

Shelly shyly raised her paw. "I might," she purred. "If Coral and Angel will sing with me."

Coral patted Shelly's shoulder. "Shelly is a great singer," she said.

"She sounds like Kelpy Sharkson," Angel added.

Shelly felt her face getting hot. "No, I don't," she said. But she was smiling because she was Kelpy Sharkson's biggest fan. She knew all her songs by

heart. Sometimes she
dreamed about being a
singer like Kelpy when
she grew up.

"I hope you girls do
try out," Ms. Harbor
said.

"I'm not sure I'm
brave enough to sing
in front of all those
purrmaids," Shelly said.

"I hadn't thought about that," Coral
said. Sometimes, she could be a scaredy
cat. "I don't know if I'm brave enough,
either!"

Ms. Harbor swam over to Shelly
and Coral. She purred, "This year, I've
entered the Sand Sculpture Contest. I've
never sculpted sand before!"

"Aren't you scared?" Shelly asked.

Ms. Harbor smiled. "It might be scary. But it also might be an adventure!"

"And I'm here to help you two be brave," Angel added. "Nothing scares me!"

"I'll think about it," Shelly said.

"I'm sure you girls will make the right decision. But no matter what you choose to do this weekend, make sure you have fun," Ms. Harbor said. "After all, it's Founder's Day!"

The Lake family had cooked a lot of food for the Founder's Day party. It all had to be carried into the ballroom at Cove Council Hall before the guests arrived. "We're lucky you're here," Mom said.

Shelly, Angel, and Coral smiled. "I love helping you, Mom," Shelly purred.

"And we love helping Shelly!" Angel laughed.

The purrmaids began to unload the

restaurant cart. "Here, Coral," Shelly's dad called. "You take this one."

"Be careful," Angel warned. She and Shelly were already holding trays. "These are heavier than they look!"

"I can handle it, Angel," Coral said. "I don't want to spill anything."

"Especially not on Shelly," Angel teased.

Everyone knew Shelly hated to get her silky, white fur dirty, especially on a night when she was dressed up for a party.

"If you're done making fun of me," Shelly huffed, "we should get going." She frowned for a moment. But she was only pretending to be upset. She knew Angel was kidding. She tilted her head toward the open door. "Come on."

The girls swam toward the ballroom. Shelly stopped in the doorway. Even though she'd seen it before, she was always impressed. The ballroom was huge and had a high ceiling. The sand walls had been polished to a golden shine. Gleaming seashells and dazzling starfish covered the floor.

"This might be the most beautiful room in the whole world," Shelly purred.

"Let's go, Shelly," Coral said. "Your mother is waiting."

"And these trays are getting heavier!" Angel whined.

The purrmaids giggled. Mom was floating near a long table decorated with lace corals. Shelly asked, "Where do you want these?"

"Right here," Mom answered. She tapped an empty part of the table. "Is this everything?" she asked.

Shelly nodded.

"Fin-tastic!" Mom said. "We were running out of room!"

"The food looks beautiful, Mrs. Lake," Coral said.

"And delicious," Angel added.

Mom smiled. "I'm glad you think so. Everything has to be purr-fect tonight."

"It certainly appears to be purr-fect!"

boomed a voice. "I knew I could trust the Lakes to cook up a paw-sitively fabulous party meal."

Shelly turned. It was Mayor Rivers. Three purrmaids swam behind him—Adrianna, Umiko, and Cascade. Shelly wasn't surprised that they were all wearing lavender clothes. The Catfish Club *always* wore lavender, just like Shelly and her best friends always wore their friendship bracelets.

Mayor Rivers said, "This is my niece, Adrianna, and her friends, Cascade and Umiko. Do you girls know each other?"

"We're all in the same class at sea school," Shelly replied.

"Eel-Twelve, right?" Mayor Rivers asked. The girls nodded. "Wonderful! Your teacher, Ms. Harbor, is here tonight, too." He looked over the plates on the table. "Now, I have an important question. What should I try first?"

"Here, try this," Shelly suggested as she held out a plate. "It's a new sushi roll Mom invented. It's called a Garden Urchin Roll."

Umiko, Cascade, and Adrianna each took one piece of the sushi. But Mayor Rivers stuffed a paw-ful into his mouth. "Mmmm," he purred. "This is good! What's in it?"

"Sea urchin," Mrs. Lake answered, "and all sorts of sea vegetables."

The moment she said *vegetables,* the mayor's face turned green. "You mean . . . it's . . . it's . . . *healthy*?"

Everyone giggled. "If you want something sweet," Shelly said, "we have coconut pie over there."

Mayor Rivers reached for the pie. Then

he stopped. "I shouldn't," he mumbled. "Mrs. Rivers wouldn't like it if I had dessert before dinner." He sighed. "I should make my big announcement now."

The mayor floated onto the stage and tapped the microphone to get everyone's attention. "Welcome, friends. Thank you for coming tonight," he said. "Before you enjoy this fin-credible party, there's one thing I'd like to say."

"Shush, everyone!" Adrianna snapped. "My uncle, the mayor, is about to give an important speech."

"Actually," Cascade whispered, "I think it's a quick announcement, not a whole speech."

Adrianna scowled. Shelly lowered her face so the Catfish Club wouldn't see her smiling.

Mayor Rivers continued, "I hope

many of you will consider trying out for a spot in our community showcase. We want to hear different voices celebrating our town. Every purrmaid in the showcase will get to purr-form with this year's special guest." He waved for someone to swim closer. "I know you're all excited to meet our guest."

The purrmaid had shiny golden fur and beautiful green eyes. She wore a deep blue coat over a silver top. The coat was dotted with shimmering sea glass shaped like music notes. She carried a guitar in one paw and waved at the crowd with the other.

Shelly knew who she was right away, even before Mayor Rivers announced, "I'm thrilled to introduce you all to . . . Kelpy Sharkson!"

"Shelly!" Angel gasped. "Now you *have* to sing in the showcase tomorrow!"

"You'll get to sing with Kelpy Sharkson!" Coral exclaimed.

Shelly nodded. "Will you help me?" she asked. "I can't do it alone."

"Of course!" Angel replied.

"What are friends for?" Coral added.

"This might be the best Founder's Day ever!" Shelly laughed.

Shelly hardly slept after the party. She was too excited about meeting Kelpy Sharkson! Somehow, she woke up in the morning full of energy. Her older sisters, Tempest and Gale, were still sleeping. Shelly tried to get ready quietly.

As she brushed her fur, she sang softly.

♫ *Na na* ♪ *na na* ♪ *na na* ♫
♫ *Na na* ♪ *na na* ♪ *na na* ♫

Someone asked, "Is that the new Kelpy Sharkson song?"

Shelly turned to face the voice. "Did I wake you, Tempest?"

"Yes," Tempest mumbled.

"You woke me, too," Gale grumbled.

"I'm sorry," Shelly said.

Gale rubbed her eyes. "Is she right? Were you singing 'Castaway'?"

Shelly nodded. Even though "Cast-away" was brand-new, she already knew all the words.

"You have such a great voice," Tempest said.

"I wish I sounded like you!" Gale added.

Shelly blushed. "Thank you," she purred.

"Are you going to try out for the showcase this year?" Gale asked.

Shelly grinned. "Yes!"

"Paw-some!" Tempest said.

"I hope you get in," Gale said. She pulled the blankets over her head. "For now, though, please get out!"

Shelly laughed. She swam out of the bedroom and closed the door so her sisters could sleep. She found her parents in the kitchen. Dad was dressed, but Mom was still in her pajamas. "Good morning!" she called.

"You're up early," Mom mumbled.

"It's Founder's Day!" Shelly laughed. "There's so much to do! I can't wait!"

"You're dressed and everything," Dad said. Usually, Shelly took a long time to get ready. She had to make sure that every last detail was purr-fect, and purr-fection took time.

Shelly twirled around. "Do you like my outfit?" she asked.

"You look beautiful, Shelly," Mom replied.

Dad nodded. "I agree."

"I'm meeting Angel and Coral in Meow Meadow at nine o'clock," Shelly said.

"I'm going to Meow Meadow, too,"

Dad said. "Are you taking the dance lesson?"

Shelly shook her head. "We decided to audition for the showcase," she explained.

"That's fin-tastic!" Mom exclaimed. "Good luck!"

"Thanks, Mom," Shelly purred. "But luck isn't as important as practice. And that's why we're meeting early. We're going to practice all day!"

Dad and Shelly waved goodbye to Mom and swam off. Meow Meadow was filled with purrmaids celebrating Founder's Day. Shelly spied Ms. Harbor's rainbow fur in the crowd of purrmaids. She was dancing with Mr. Shippley, the sea school librarian.

Shelly had never seen her teachers dance. Ms. Harbor was twisting and twirling as fast as she could. But Mr. Shippley only rocked slowly to the left and then to the right. He kept checking the watch on his wrist like he couldn't wait for the song to end.

"They look a little silly, don't they?" Dad said.

"Grown-ups always do when they dance!" Shelly replied.

Dad scowled. "Even me?" he asked.

Shelly tried to look serious while she shook her head. But she giggled. Dad said, "I'll show you. When I'm done practicing, I'll be the best dancer you've ever seen!"

"Maybe you can dance to my song at the showcase!" Shelly laughed. Dad stuck his tongue out and then swam away.

Shelly looked for her friends on the other side of Meow Meadow. The park was full of families with little kittens. Coral's mother and her little brother,

Shrimp, were there. *That means Coral should be here, too,* Shelly thought.

But when Shelly searched the crowd, she didn't see Coral anywhere. There was no sign of Angel, either. She tapped her tail against the sand and scratched her

head. *Where are they?* she wondered. She looked up at the clock tower on Cove Council Hall. "It's only eight forty-five!" she groaned. Her friends wouldn't be there for another fifteen minutes.

Shelly decided to hang out in the gazebo. *I'll sing to pass the time until nine o'clock,* she thought.

♫ *Na na ♪ na na ♪ na na ♫*
♫ *Na na ♪ na na ♪ na na ♫*

Shelly sang "Seas by Seas." Then she sang "Purrmaids Like Us," "Since You've Been Swimming," and "A Moment Like Fish." By the time she finished "Castaway," she finally spotted Angel and Coral. They waved, and their bracelets sparkled in the light.

"Shelly!" Angel shouted. "You're late!"

"Late?" Shelly replied, frowning. "What are you talking about?"

"You said you'd meet us by nine," Coral said.

Shelly spun around and looked up at the clock tower again. The short hand of the clock pointed at the nine. But the long hand pointed at the three. "It's nine fifteen!" Shelly gasped. "I guess I lost track of time while I was singing."

Coral giggled. "We should have known singing had something to do with this."

"I'm glad we found you," Angel said. "We have just enough time to get to the library."

The historical tour of Kittentail Cove started at the library. Every Founder's Day, the girls took the tour. But this year was different—at least for Shelly. "I was hoping we could sign up for the show-case," she said. "And then I wanted to practice our song." She bit her lip. "You both purr-omised."

"Oh, Shelly," Coral cooed, "we're not taking the tour."

Angel put a paw around Shelly's shoulders. "But we have to go to the library right away."

"I don't understand," Shelly said. "How will the library help with the showcase?"

"The sign-ups are at the library!" Coral announced.

"We even thought about where to practice," Angel said. "We're going to the P.A.W."

"There are practice rooms there that we can use," Coral added.

Shelly smiled. "I should have known you two would never let me down," she purred, and hugged her friends.

The girls swam to the Kittentail Cove Library.

There was a new sign on the librarian's desk. It read:

Founder's Day Showcase
SIGN UP HERE
Tryouts begin at 4:00 PM
Showcase begins at 7:00 PM

A crowd of purrmaids floated around the desk, waiting. "Is everyone here signing up for the showcase tryouts?" Shelly asked.

The striped purrmaid behind Angel said, "That's why I'm here."

"Me too," someone else said.

Shelly gulped. *This is a purr-oblem,* she thought. *I'm not a better singer than everyone here!*

"I didn't realize so many purrmaids would sign up," Coral whispered.

"How many tryouts can they even fit in today?" Angel asked.

The striped purrmaid said, "I heard that everyone who signs up before nine-thirty gets a turn."

Shelly looked at the clock above the library door. "It's nine twenty-five now!"

"At least we're almost to the sign-up sheet," Coral said.

When Shelly turned around, there were three purrmaids in front of her!

"Excuse me," Shelly huffed. "We were here first."

The three purrmaids spun around. It was the Catfish Club! "Of course, it's the three of you cutting the line. *Again*," Angel grumbled.

"This isn't like the museum," Adrianna purred. "There's definitely no line here."

"That still doesn't mean you can push to wherever you want!" Coral yowled.

It looked like the girls would get into an argument. Luckily, the librarian behind the desk interrupted them. "Do you girls want to sign up?" she asked. "There's just a little time left."

"Yes!" yelped Shelly and Adrianna at the same time.

The librarian held out a sea pen. "Hurry up, then."

Shelly reached for the sea pen. But Adrianna snatched it first. Shelly narrowed her eyes and took the sea pen when Adrianna was done.

"We're all signed up!" Umiko said.

"Just in time, too," Coral added.

"So there was nothing to worry about," Angel said.

"And nothing to fight about," Cascade said.

Shelly sighed. "I guess you're right."

"We're all going to get a turn," Adrianna said. She pointed to the large crowd of other purrmaids who had also signed up. "I just don't know if it will make a difference."

Shelly felt butterfly fish flutter in her tummy. "Are you nervous?" she asked.

Adrianna gulped. "Mr. Boatman is over there," she said. "He's our music teacher! He's got to be better than us."

Cascade said, "My aunt Marlene is trying out, too. She was an opera singer in college."

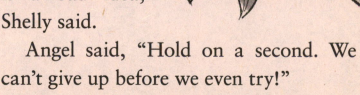

"Maybe this is a bad idea," Shelly said.

Angel said, "Hold on a second. We can't give up before we even try!"

"Remember what Ms. Harbor told us?" Cascade asked. "She said this could be an adventure. So all this competition isn't a purr-oblem. It's really a challenge!"

"I think Angel and Cascade are right," Umiko said. Suddenly, her eyes grew wide. "I just had an idea!" she exclaimed.

"What is it?" Adrianna asked.

"Remember when we did the art project together?" Umiko began. The others nodded. "We worked together on that, and it was fin-tastic. Maybe you three could sing with us."

"That's a paw-some idea!" Angel said. "We could all go to the P.A.W. and rehearse."

"We've been practicing 'Purrmaids Like Us' by Kelpy Sharkson," Adrianna said. "Do you know that song?"

"Know it?" Shelly shouted. "I love that song! I could sing it in my sleep."

Adrianna grinned. "Fin-tastic! You three can be backup singers."

Shelly scowled. "I don't sing backup," she grumbled.

"Shelly's too good for that!" Angel added.

"But we've been practicing for a while," Adrianna said. "The tryouts are in a few hours. We don't have time to fit in another lead singer!"

"We haven't actually practiced much," Cascade said.

"And," Umiko said, "the one time we did sing . . . we didn't sound that good."

Adrianna frowned. "We *could* use some help," she said.

"What if Adrianna and Shelly both sang the lead parts of 'Purrmaids Like Us'?" Coral said. "The rest of us could be your backup."

Shelly shrugged. "I'm fine with that," she said.

"I guess I am, too," Adrianna replied.

"Great!" Angel exclaimed. "Let's hurry to the P.A.W. and get to work."

"Last one there is a rotten skeg!" Cascade called.

The girls laughed and raced to the P.A.W. When they arrived, there was only one practice room left that wasn't filled with singers. "I guess everyone had the same idea," Umiko said.

"You know what they say," Shelly replied. "Practice makes purr-fect!"

The practice room had a large golden harp in one corner, so it was barely big enough to fit all six girls. "I guess it's good that we're working together," Cascade said, "or else we'd be fighting over this room!"

"I'm glad we won't be wasting time arguing," Adrianna said. "We need to

start practicing right now." She led the girls through the open door of the empty room.

"I agree," Angel said. "When we're done, we can go to the Sand Sculpture Contest at sea school."

"Don't forget about lunch!" Coral yowled. "There's a picnic today in Leondra's Square."

"And the Founder's Day parade!" Umiko added.

Adrianna scowled. "I don't know if we have time for all that."

"But I want to go to the Sand Sculpture Contest, too," Umiko moaned.

"I'm hungry already," Cascade whined.

"And we can't miss the parade!" Angel said.

Shelly didn't think they should do anything except rehearse until the tryouts. But she knew her friends loved everything about Founder's Day. "Let's just get started," she suggested. "Maybe we will be ready quickly." She floated in front of the harp, ready to play.

Adrianna handed out copies of the song. "Here are your parts," she said to Angel, Coral, Umiko, and Cascade. She brought a copy over to Shelly at the harp. "And here's ours."

Shelly counted out the beat. "One . . . two . . . one, two, three, four!" The girls began to sing.

♫ *Purrmaids like us just have to swim together.* ♫
♫ *Stick with your friends through calm or stormy weather.* ♫

Unfortunately, they didn't sound very musical!

After another minute, Shelly stopped

playing. She waved her paws to get her
friends' attention. "Everybody, let's take
a break," she said.

"What's wrong?" Coral asked.

Shelly bit her lip. She thought, *How can I tell my friends that they're not singing well?*

Adrianna cleared her throat. "We're not all singing with the same beat." She floated over to Umiko and Cascade. "You two were singing too fast," she said. "You finished your lines before I was halfway done." Then she turned to Coral and Angel. "And you two were singing too slowly."

"I thought there was something wrong," Umiko said. "The song didn't sound right."

"Actually," Cascade said, "it sounded really *wrong.*"

"How do we make sure we're all singing with the same beat?" Coral asked.

"I'll clap my paws," Adrianna suggested. "One clap for every beat."

"And I can tap my tail on the ground," Shelly added. "Let's try again." She started tapping her tail. Adrianna clapped and signaled for the girls to begin singing.

♫ *Oh whoa oh* ♪ *oh whoa oh* ♫

This time, everyone sang with the same beat. But it still didn't sound like beautiful music!

Adrianna stopped singing. She put her face in her paws. Shelly didn't need to ask what was bothering her. She could hear it for herself. Her friends were singing loudly—but completely off-key!

Shelly took her paws off the harp strings again. "Listen up, everyone!" she shouted.

"Are we still getting the beat wrong?" Coral asked.

Shelly shook her head. "No, the beat was fine this time," she replied.

"The purr-oblem is that you four don't know the notes!" Adrianna snapped. "Angel and Umiko, your singing is flat. Coral and Cascade, your voices are too sharp!"

Coral sighed. "We're doing our best."

"We're never going to get a spot in the showcase like this," Adrianna grumbled.

Shelly saw her friends frown. She had to do something. "I know!" she exclaimed. "We should sing some scales. That will help us with the notes *and* the beat."

"What's a scale?" Umiko asked.

Shelly explained, "A scale is a set of eight notes that go together in a certain order."

"If you learn the proper notes in a scale, you won't sing too high or too low," Adrianna added.

"That's a good idea!" Coral said.

"We probably should have started with scales," Cascade agreed.

Shelly nodded. "We'll fix that right now," she purred. "I'll play the notes on the harp. You sing the same note that I play." She looked her friends over, head to tail. "Everyone, straighten your backs," she said. "Relax your shoulders. Keep your paws at your sides. Breathe in slowly." She played the first note. "Now let's sing!" Then she played a scale as they sang along.

♫ *La la* ♪ *la la* ♪ *la la* ♪ *la la* ♫

"Hey, that didn't sound too bad!" Adrianna said.

Shelly said, "Let's do another one."

The girls took a deep breath and waited for Shelly to start. They sang the notes of the scale. When they finished, Shelly cheered, "That was really great!"

"So are we done with scales?" Cascade asked.

"Not yet," Adrianna said. "We should sing a few more."

Shelly thought she heard her friends sighing. But she ignored that and played the harp again.

The girls sang five more scales. After the last one, Adrianna clapped. "No one was singing out of tune or off beat!" she exclaimed.

"Could we be done practicing, then?" Coral asked. "I'm getting hungry."

Shelly shrugged. "We still need to run through the actual song," she said.

Angel pointed to the clock. "Can we hurry? The picnic has already started. I'm starving!"

"We can't skip lunch," Umiko said.

Shelly sighed. "We're really not ready for the tryout yet. But I guess we do have to eat."

"We can grab a quick meal," Adrianna

said, "but then we'll come right back
to practice."

The other girls didn't look too happy
about that. *They're probably just hungry,*

Shelly thought. She held the door open and said, "Come on."

When they got to Leondra's Square, Shelly and Cascade grabbed sea cucumber and seaweed wraps. Coral and Umiko chose oyster rolls. Angel and Adrianna decided to skip right to dessert. They nibbled on chocolate chip starfish bars.

"This is exactly what I needed!" Angel laughed.

"Everything is so yummy!" Umiko exclaimed.

Shelly nodded and took the last bite of her wrap. She wiped her paws and announced, "I'm done."

"Me too," said Adrianna. "Time to get back to the P.A.W."

Coral scowled. "I'm not done."

Cascade still had a mouthful of food.

She swallowed quickly and said, "I'm still hungry."

"And we want to go to the Sand Sculpture Contest," Angel added. "We told you that."

"But we need to keep rehearsing until we sound purr-fect," Adrianna said.

"That means we have to go back now," Shelly said. "And we might stay there all day."

Coral, Angel, Cascade, and Umiko looked at each other. "This is turning into the worst Founder's Day ever," Angel grumbled.

"What are you talking about?" Adrianna asked. "You all agreed to try out for the showcase, didn't you?"

The four girls nodded.

Shelly said, "That takes a lot of work."

"We didn't think it was going to be *this much* work," Umiko moaned.

"We thought it would be fun," Coral added, "but this is hard."

"We're just doing the same thing over and over," Cascade whined.

"It's getting a little boring," Angel muttered. "And you two are being bossy."

Shelly crossed her paws. "This is our one chance to sing with Kelpy Sharkson," she said. "We can't stop now!"

"We've been doing everything you and Adrianna have been ordering us to do all day!" Coral groaned. "Can't we do something else for a while?"

"We can do something else when we get the song right!" Adrianna said.

"What about what we want?" Cascade asked.

Shelly shrugged. "If we want the song to be purr-fect, we don't have time for anything except practicing."

"But you two don't even like the way we sing," Angel snapped. "Maybe it would be better if you went to the tryouts without us."

Shelly's eyes grew wide. "But you're my friends," she said. "I want to do this *with* you."

"Me too," Adrianna added.

One by one, Umiko, Coral, Angel, and Cascade looked down at the ground. Finally, Coral said, "You're both better singers than we are. You'll do better at the tryouts without us."

"And you two want to sing at the showcase a lot more than we do," Cascade said. "We want to do other things today."

Shelly gulped. "If you really want to do something else," she said, "I guess you should."

Adrianna nodded.

"I knew you'd understand!" Angel squealed. She swam over to hug Shelly so quickly that she spun them both around.

The other girls grinned. They didn't notice that Shelly and Adrianna weren't smiling.

"Good luck this afternoon!" Coral called.

"We know you'll do a great job!" Umiko said.

"We'd better go," Cascade said. "The Sand Sculpture Contest is about to start."

Cascade, Angel, Umiko, and Coral waved as they swam away. "We'll see you later!" Angel called over her shoulder.

Shelly turned to Adrianna. "I guess it's just you and me," she gulped.

Adrianna slowly nodded. "I guess so," she said. "We can do this, right?"

Shelly squared her shoulders. "Yes, we can," she declared. "You're a great singer."

"You are, too," Adrianna said.

"Let's go back to the P.A.W. and turn our song into a duet," Shelly said.

Adrianna said, "We'll practice until . . ."

". . . it's purr-fect!" both girls said together.

Shelly smiled. "We'd better get started!"

The girls hurried back to the P.A.W. "I hope there's still a room for us," Shelly said.

But there was nothing to worry about. When the girls got there, most of the practice rooms were empty.

"What happened to everyone?" Adrianna wondered.

Just then, Mr. Boatman swam through the door of one of the rooms. "Hello, girls! Are you here to practice?"

Shelly nodded. "It was so crowded here before lunch," she said. "Where did everyone go?"

"I think most purrmaids practiced

their purr-formances this morning. Then they left to enjoy Founder's Day," Mr. Boatman said.

"How can they be ready?" Adrianna asked. "Shouldn't they keep rehearsing all day?"

Mr. Boatman scratched his head. "You can always practice more, I suppose," he answered. "The more you practice, the better you get at something. But being purr-fect isn't the only thing that matters. I'm going to meet up with my family at sea school to watch the Sand Sculpture Contest. I don't want to miss all the fun!"

Shelly and Adrianna looked at each other. "Our song isn't good enough yet," Adrianna said.

Mr. Boatman purred, "I've heard you both sing in class. You're great. I bet you could have some fun this afternoon and your tryout will still be paw-some."

Shelly shook her head. "You don't understand," she said. "This is our chance to sing with Kelpy Sharkson. We can't stop working now!"

Mr. Boatman nodded. "You girls have made your decision," he said. "Good luck!"

Shelly swam straight to the harp in their practice room. "Now that it's just the two of us, I think we should sing slower," she said. "That way we can really show off our voices."

"I don't think so," Adrianna said. "This song sounds a lot better with a fast beat."

Shelly frowned. "I don't want to waste time arguing," she said. "We can try it both ways. Then we can decide which way sounds better."

"Fine," Adrianna replied. "Let's sing it fast first."

Shelly rolled her eyes. "Fine," she huffed. *I know I'm right,* she thought. *Adrianna will see that in a minute.*

The girls started singing. But before they finished the first verse, Adrianna said, "This doesn't sound right."

Shelly smiled. She thought, *I knew it!* But there was no reason to rub it in. "I'll start again," she purred. "This time, we'll go slower."

The girls sang the first verse of the song again. Now it was Shelly who stopped them. "This isn't right, either!" she exclaimed.

Shelly and Adrianna sang and sang. After an hour, Shelly swam away from the harp. Her shoulders slumped. "It still doesn't sound right to me," she moaned.

"You're right," Adrianna sighed.

"We've tried everything!" Shelly yowled. "You singing the high part, me singing the high part . . ."

"Singing faster, singing slower,"

Adrianna continued. "But nothing is working."

"We need help," Shelly grumbled. "I wish our friends were still here."

"Do you know what the worst part is?" Adrianna asked.

"That singing isn't even fun like this?" Shelly said.

Adrianna nodded. "We should just give up," she said. "We'll never get a spot in the showcase. We'll just sound silly next to all the other singers."

Shelly hung her head. "Maybe you're right," she mumbled. She floated to the door and opened it to leave.

But then Shelly's ears pricked up. "Wait!" she gasped. "Do you hear that?"

Someone was in the practice room next door. The door wasn't completely closed.

Shelly could hear a guitar strumming out a very familiar tune.

♫ *I'll flip my fins* ♪ *and I'll swim through the sea.* ♫
♫ *I'll care for my friends* ♪ *the way they care for me.* ♫

The voice made Shelly freeze.
"What's wrong?" Adrianna asked.
"Nothing," Shelly purred. "Nothing's

wrong at all." She spun around to face Adrianna. "Do you know who that is?"

Adrianna shrugged.

Shelly grabbed Adrianna's paw and pulled her into the hall. "That's Kelpy Sharkson!"

"How do you know?" Adrianna asked.

Shelly grinned. She couldn't count how many hours she'd listened to Kelpy's music. "I would know her voice anywhere in the ocean!" she replied.

"What should we do?" Adrianna wondered. "Should we go meet her?"

"I can't be this close to Kelpy Sharkson and not say hello!" Shelly cried.

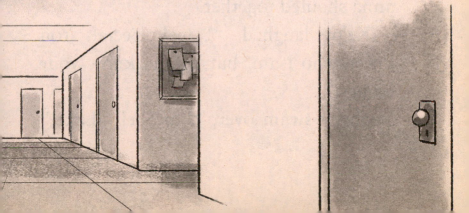

Adrianna nodded. "You're right. We can tell her the mayor is my uncle. Then she won't mind us introducing ourselves."

Shelly and Adrianna peeked in through the small gap in the door. They watched Kelpy finish the song. As soon as she strummed out the last note, the girls clapped.

"That was really wonderful!" Shelly exclaimed.

"You're amazing!" Adrianna added.

Kelpy smiled. "Thank you!" she purred. "I didn't know I had an audience. I'm—"

"Kelpy Sharkson!" Shelly and Adrianna shouted together.

Kelpy laughed. "I feel special. You know who I am, but I don't know your names."

Shelly swam over. "I'm Shelly Lake,"

she said, shaking Kelpy's paw. Then she looked back at her classmate. "And that's Adrianna Rivers," she added.

"Nice to meet you both," Kelpy said. "Shelly, do you know the chefs at Lake Restaurant?"

"They're my parents!" Shelly replied.

"The food at the party was so good!" Kelpy cooed. "My favorite was the Garden Urchin Roll. Yummy—and healthy!" She smiled at Shelly. "Your family did a paw-some job."

"And my uncle, the mayor, did a good job, too," Adrianna said. "He was in charge of finding the chefs for the party."

"Yes, I suppose he did," Kelpy agreed. She put her guitar down. "Was I singing too loud?" she asked. "Did I bother you?"

"No way!" Shelly cried. "We were done practicing."

"Are you ready for the showcase try-outs?" Kelpy asked.

Shelly shook her head. Adrianna said, "We were going to try out. But now we can't."

"Oh no!" Kelpy replied. "What happened?"

Shelly bit her lip. "We were going to sing with our friends," she explained. "But they said we were taking the fun out of it."

"Actually, they said we were ordering them around." Adrianna shrugged. "I guess I can be a little bossy. Sometimes."

Shelly giggled. "Just sometimes?"

Adrianna frowned. But Shelly put a paw on her shoulder. "Don't worry," she said. "I can be purr-ty bossy, too. I just think things should be done the right way, and that's usually . . ."

"... *my* way!" both girls exclaimed together.

Shelly turned back to Kelpy. "When we tried to sing by ourselves, it didn't sound right."

"Not my way *or* her way," Adrianna added.

"So we're giving up," Shelly said. She stared at her tail and tried to keep from crying.

"Hmmm," Kelpy said. "Would you like some advice?"

Shelly's head snapped up. Advice? From a real star purr-former? "Yes, please!"

"Here's the thing about music," Kelpy explained. "It's supposed to make you happy and bring purrmaids together. You feel the songs you love with your heart more than you hear them with your ears."

"Is that why music makes you feel less lonely, even when you're alone?" Adrianna asked.

"And why a song feels different when

you're by yourself instead of with your friends?" Shelly asked.

Kelpy nodded. "Exactly! Both of you understand. Most of the time, I think music sounds better when I'm with friends."

"I agree," Adrianna said.

"I think as long as you're not having fun or feeling happy, the song isn't going to sound right to you," Kelpy said.

Kelpy's advice made a lot of sense. Shelly thought about things that were fun and made her happy. Suddenly, she realized what she and Adrianna were doing wrong. She purred, "Thank you so much, Kelpy. You helped me figure out how to make our song purr-fect."

"What?" Adrianna asked. "How?"

"I'll show you in a minute," Shelly answered.

Shelly tried to shake Kelpy's paw again.

But Kelpy pulled her into a hug. "You're welcome," Kelpy said. "I'm glad I could help!"

"We'll see you later!" Shelly said. "Come on, Adrianna! I know what we have to do!"

Shelly zipped through Kittentail Cove as fast as she could swim.

"Slow down," Adrianna begged.

"We're almost there!" Shelly shouted.

"Where are we going?" Adrianna asked.

Shelly smiled over her shoulder. "To sea school," she replied. "To find what was missing from our song."

"Of course!" Adrianna said. "That's where our friends are! They're the missing part."

It only took a few more minutes for Shelly and Adrianna to reach sea school.

The Sand Sculpture Contest was under way. This year's theme was Enchanting Creatures of the Land. Groups of purrmaids worked on their creations. Shelly saw a lion, a hippopotamus, a giraffe, and even a human!

Shelly looked right and left, trying to spot their friends.

"I hope they're still here," Adrianna purred.

"I see Ms. Harbor over there," Shelly said. Their teacher was working on a pile of sand. It didn't look like much more than a blob.

"Maybe she's seen the girls," Adrianna said.

But before they could swim toward Ms. Harbor, someone said, "Aren't you two supposed to be practicing at the P.A.W.?"

Shelly would know Kelpy Sharkson's voice anywhere in the ocean. But she would know the voice she just heard anywhere in the entire universe. She spun around and squealed, "Angel!"

"Not just Angel," Coral said. "Umiko, Cascade, and I are all here, too."

"But what are *you* doing here?" Cascade asked.

"We were looking for you," Shelly replied. "We wanted to know if we could spend the rest of Founder's Day with you."

"What about trying out for the showcase?" Coral asked.

Shelly and Adrianna shrugged. "We'd love to go to the tryouts," Adrianna said.

"But we'd rather sing with you while we enjoy Founder's Day than sing by ourselves onstage," Shelly said.

Angel, Coral, Cascade, and Umiko looked at each other. Then Umiko said, "You're lucky you found us here. We were just about to leave."

"Can we come with you?" Adrianna asked.

"Yes, you can," Angel answered. "We're going back to the P.A.W."

Shelly's eyes grew wide. "I don't understand," she said.

Cascade said, "We realized that we haven't been very good friends. We didn't help you rehearse the way we should have."

"We get to go to Founder's Day events every year," Coral said.

"But this might be your only chance to sing with Kelpy Sharkson," Angel continued. "Even though we aren't very good singers, we want to support you."

"Is there anything we can do to help?" Coral asked.

Shelly reached for Coral's paw and Angel's paw. Adrianna did the same with Umiko and Cascade. The girls floated in a circle, holding paws. "We're lucky to have great friends like you," Shelly said.

"Well," said Angel, "luck isn't as

important as practice. We need to get back to the P.A.W. so you two can finish practicing."

Adrianna shook her head. "We're not singing without you," she purred.

"But we're terrible singers," Umiko said.

"We won't do a good job," Coral said.

Shelly smiled. "Everything is better when we're with our friends," she declared.

Adrianna nodded. "Shelly and I would rather sing with you than do a solo," she added.

"Actually," Cascade whispered, "it's not a solo if both of you sing. It's a duet."

That made the girls giggle.

"So," Shelly asked, "will you sing with us?"

"We really want you to," Adrianna said.

"Even if that means we probably won't win a spot in the showcase?" Angel asked.

"If we're all together," Shelly purred, "we've already won."

Back in the practice room, the girls sang "Purrmaids Like Us." They had so much fun that they sang "A Moment Like Fish." Then "Since You've Been Swimming."

A dozen songs later, the girls were out of breath. "Just one more?" Shelly asked. "I want to sing 'Castaway.'"

"We can't say no to that!" Adrianna laughed.

As soon as they finished the last note of

the song, someone clapped and shouted, "That was fin-credible!"

It only took a moment for everyone to recognize the purrmaid at the door. "Kelpy Sharkson!" Umiko gasped.

"I can't believe it!" Cascade exclaimed.

"We love your music!" Coral said.

Kelpy grinned. "Thank you!" she said. "I was looking for my friends Shelly and Adrianna when I heard you singing. You're really good!"

Shelly said, "I think we're finally ready for the tryouts!"

Kelpy's grin disappeared. "The tryouts are over," she said.

"*What?*" Adrianna yelped. "We missed them? This is a cat-tastrophe!"

Shelly checked the clock on the wall. "We must have lost track of time," she moaned.

"I can't believe how late it is," Angel
groaned.

"We were having such a good time,
I never even looked at the clock," Coral
said.

"Me neither," Umiko added.

Shelly squeezed her eyes shut so the
tears wouldn't fall.

Then Cascade said, "We did have a lot of fun, though."

Shelly looked up. "You're right, Cascade," she said. "We *did* have fun."

"A lot more fun than we had earlier," Adrianna agreed.

The other girls smiled and nodded. Shelly said, "So far, singing with all of you has been my favorite part of Founder's Day."

"Then you girls didn't miss much!" Kelpy purred. "If singing together made you happy, you figured out how to do it right."

"And if anyone knows how to sing the right way, it's Kelpy Sharkson!" Angel said.

Everyone laughed. Then Adrianna said, "Still, it would have been nice to sing in front of everyone."

Shelly nodded. "You're right, Adrianna," she said.

"You two would have been great," Coral said.

"No," Umiko said, "you two would have been *paw-some*."

"All six of you are paw-sitively amazing!" Kelpy exclaimed. "You know, I *am* the star tonight," she said. "I could make you all my backup singers. Then you can still purr-form at the showcase. We just need to leave soon to make it to dress rehearsal."

Shelly felt butterfly fish fluttering in her tummy again. Singing with Kelpy Sharkson would be a dream come true. But when she opened her mouth, she didn't say yes. Instead, she said, "I don't think we should do that."

"What do you mean?" Adrianna yelped. "Why not?"

"I don't understand," Kelpy said. "I thought this would make you happy."

Shelly exclaimed, "Oh, Kelpy! It would!"

"Then why are you saying no?" Kelpy asked.

Shelly bit her lip. "I've wanted to sing with you ever since I heard your first song, Kelpy. It would be fin-credible to be onstage with you." She took a deep breath. "But I don't think it would be fair to all the purrmaids who tried out for the showcase."

"I can't believe I'm saying this *again*," Adrianna said, "but Shelly's right. I really wanted to be in the showcase, too. But there were other purrmaids who deserve this chance. They followed the rules."

"And it really is better to follow the rules," Coral said.

Shelly giggled. Of course, Coral would still be thinking about rules!

"So what are we going to do instead?" Umiko asked.

"We could just stay here and keep singing," Cascade suggested.

Shelly looked at the clock again. "If we aren't singing in the showcase," she said, "we don't have to go to dress rehearsal. That means we have time to do some other Founder's Day activities before the show."

"I have another idea," Kelpy said. "A lot of purrmaids wouldn't care about what's fair or what the rules say. Most would just think about what was best for them. Only really paw-some purrmaids would give up their dreams just to do what's right." She smiled and picked up her guitar. "I really like to sing with paw-some purrmaids." She strummed her guitar strings. "Would you sing with me before I have to go to dress rehearsal?"

Shelly's mouth dropped open. She didn't know what to say. She turned to Adrianna. She was speechless, too.

Coral put her paw on Shelly's elbow. "The rules don't say you can't sing with Kelpy before the show," she said.

"Actually," Cascade whispered, "the rules don't say *anything* about before the show."

"What do you think, Shelly?" Adrianna asked.

Shelly twirled around with excitement. "I think," she announced, "we should start singing now so Kelpy isn't late for her purr-formance!"

The purrmaids formed a circle. Kelpy began the song. Soon all the girls had joined in.

♫ *Purrmaids like us just have to swim together.* ♫
♫ *Stick with your friends through calm or stormy weather.* ♫
♫ *Oh whoa oh ♪ oh whoa oh* ♫
♫ *Swimming with the purrmaids like us ♪ the purrmaids like us.* ♫

By the time the song ended, Shelly's face hurt from smiling so hard. "This was a real star purr-formance!" she declared. Everyone clapped for each other.

"Thank you, girls," Kelpy said. "This was so much fun." She searched her guitar case. "I want to give you something so you'll always remember me."

"We could never forget you!" Shelly exclaimed.

Kelpy smiled. "Still, I have a present."

She held out her paw. She was holding some sea-glass music notes from her blue coat. "There are, like, a million of these on my coat," she explained, "and they're always falling off. Would you like to keep them as a reminder of today?"

Each girl took one of the notes. "We could make these into necklaces!" Adrianna said.

"And we could add these to our friendship bracelets!" Angel added.

"So you like them?" Kelpy asked.

"We *love* them," Shelly replied. "Thank you so much!" She gave Kelpy a hug and whispered, "This is definitely the best Founder's Day ever!"

Read on for a peek at the Purrmaids' next adventure!

Dear Coral,

My family and I are camping in Ponyfish Grotto on the edge of Tortoiseshell Reef this week. I know that is close to Kittentail Cove. I thought maybe you could visit me there.

Love,
Sirena

PS I sent the same invitation to Angel and Shelly. I hope they can come, too!

"I would love to see Sirena again!" Shelly said. Angel nodded.

Coral frowned. "I want to see her again, too," she said. "But when we went to Tortoiseshell Reef, we got lost."

"That's one way to look at it," Angel replied. "But you could also say that the last time we went to Tortoiseshell Reef, we found a shipwreck, sunken treasure, and a new friend!"

Coral sighed. Angel was right. That trip really was paw-some. But it was also a little scary! "What about our homework?" Coral asked. "We need to do our scavenger hunt. We might not have enough time to finish that *and* go see Sirena."

Shelly scowled. "Our homework does come first," she said.

Angel crossed her paws and tapped her tail on the ground. Suddenly, she exclaimed, "I have a great idea!"